LEAH KOMAIKO

Aunt Elaine
Does the Dance
from Spain

Illustrated by
PETRA MATHERS

A Picture Yearling Book

Published by Dell Publishing
a division of
Bantam Doubleday Dell Publishing Group, Inc.
1540 Broadway
New York, New York 10036

For information address
Bantam Doubleday Dell Books for Young Readers,
New York, New York 10036.

ISBN: 0-440-40975-6
Reprinted by arrangement with
Doubleday Books for Young Readers

Printed in the United States of America

August 1994

3 5 7 9 10 8 6 4 2

DAN

For Libby.
¡Olé!
—LK

For Lou Ann.
¡Olé!
—PM

Spanish Words in This Book

adiós	good-bye	*hola*	hello
amigos	friends	*muy bien*	very well
¡caramba!	goodness!	*muy bonita*	very pretty
Catalina	Katy	*¡olé!*	hurrah!
¿cómo estás?	how are you?	*señorita*	miss
dos	two	*sí*	yes
Elena	Elaine	*tres*	three
gracias	thank you	*vámonos a bailar*	let's go dance

Yiddish Words in This Book

oy vey	oh brother, etc.

"Where's Elaine?
Again she's late.
The food is ice-cold on her plate!
Her dance show starts at half past eight!"

"Here I am,
your favorite aunt!"
"Sit down and eat."
"No, dear, I can't.
We must be going on our way.
So, *¡adiós!*
¡Olé!"

"*Oy vey!*"

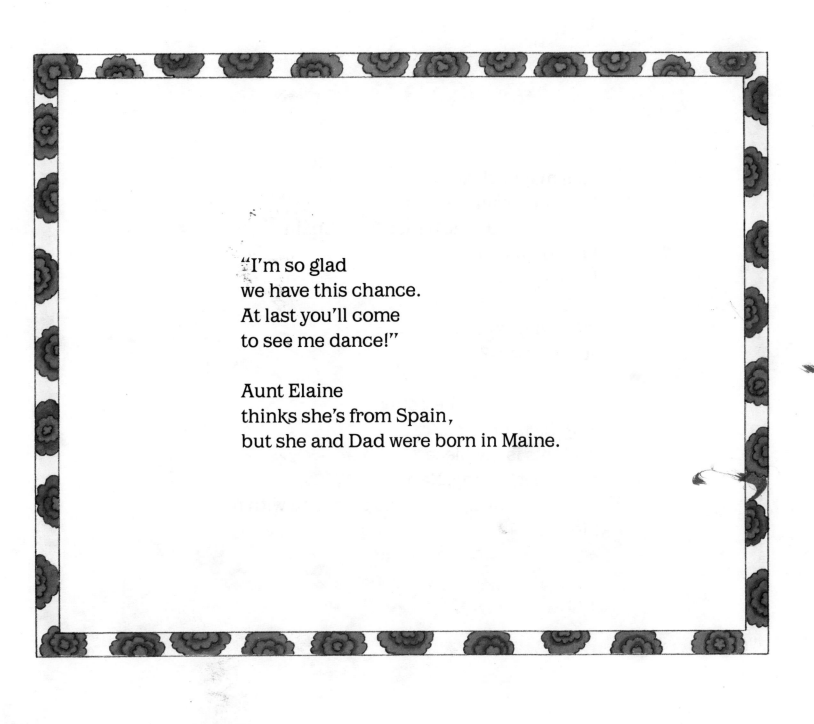

"I'm so glad
we have this chance.
At last you'll come
to see me dance!"

Aunt Elaine
thinks she's from Spain,
but she and Dad were born in Maine.

"It's magic, dear,
I can't explain
why when I do the dance from Spain
I'm not just me
I am—"

"*¡Elena! ¡Elena!*
¿Cómo estás?"

"Well, I couldn't be better.
Muy bien, gracias.
And this is my niece,
my sweet darling, Katy.
These are my *amigos* who all dance with me.
Meet...

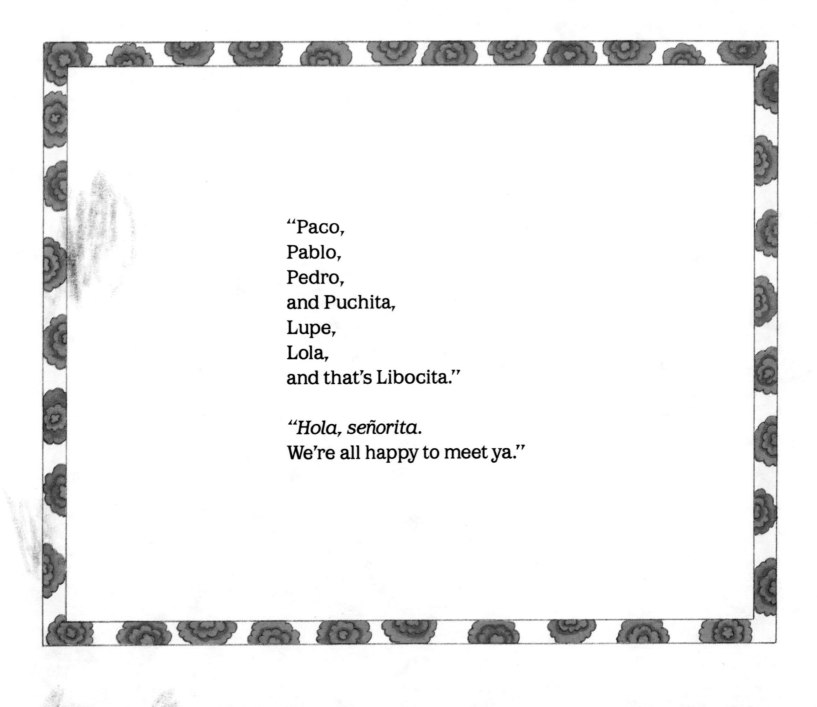

"Paco,
Pablo,
Pedro,
and Puchita,
Lupe,
Lola,
and that's Libocita."

"Hola, señorita.
We're all happy to meet ya."

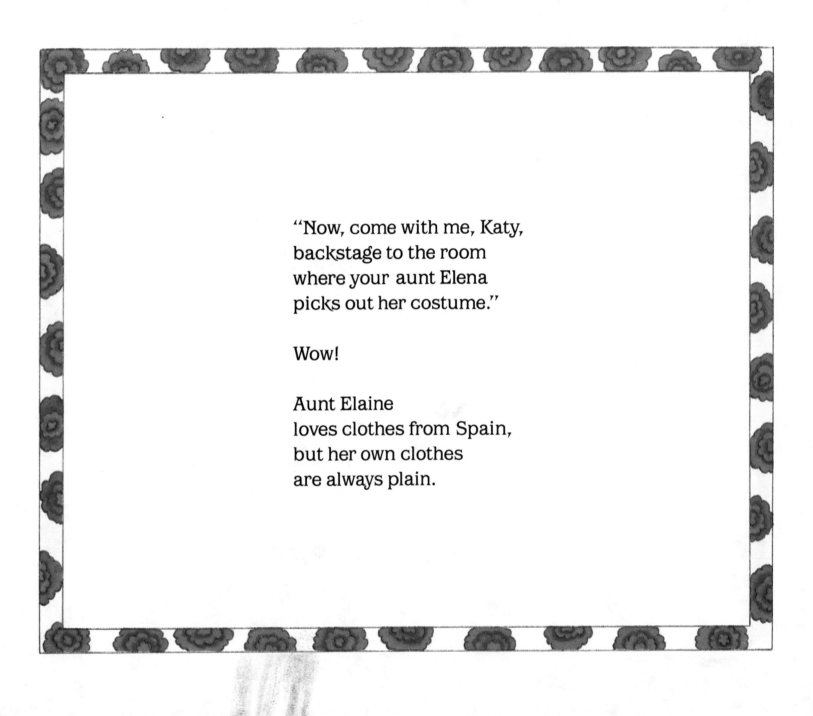

"Now, come with me, Katy,
backstage to the room
where your aunt Elena
picks out her costume."

Wow!

Aunt Elaine
loves clothes from Spain,
but her own clothes
are always plain.

"It's magic, dear,
I can't say why.
Inside this dress
I'm not me, I'm—"

"*¡Elena! ¡Elena!*
We have no time to lose.
Show starts in one minute.
Hurry, buckle your shoes.
Paco, put on your poncho.
Pedro, bring the guitar.
Castanets, everybody.
¡Vámonos a bailar!
And, girls, check your curls!"

"*Caramba,* my Katy,
This is it!
I must go.
Just walk straight out *that* door
and the usher will know
to take you to your seat
in the very first row!"

Curtain comes up.
Elaine counts,
"Dos-tres-four."
Then all the dancers stomp
a-cross-the floor.
But I don't know
where to go,
out-which-door?

Aunt Elaine
thinks she's in Spain,
so she just forgot to explain.
Now it's too late.
She can't come back.
I'll try the door
behind this rack of...

FIRST READ:
PULL HERE
PUSH THERE
PRY OPEN
CLOSE ABOVE
STEP BACK

PHOOT!

jackets
a hat
the mat-a-dor's pants.
Why does my aunt
have to do-this-dance?

1–2–3,
1–2–3,
stomp,
stomp,
stomp.

Fans
on my hands,
lashes on-my-eye,
they can't see me
with their
heads-held-high.

1–2–3,
1–2–3,
clap,
clap,
clap.

Bows
a big rose
the dress with-the-train,
all I want
is to find
Aunt-E-laine.

¡Olé,
olé,
olé!

Hey!

"Ah, *señorita,*
you look *muy bonita!*"

Then I see all the others
and in a second I know,
the dancing is over
I missed the whole show.

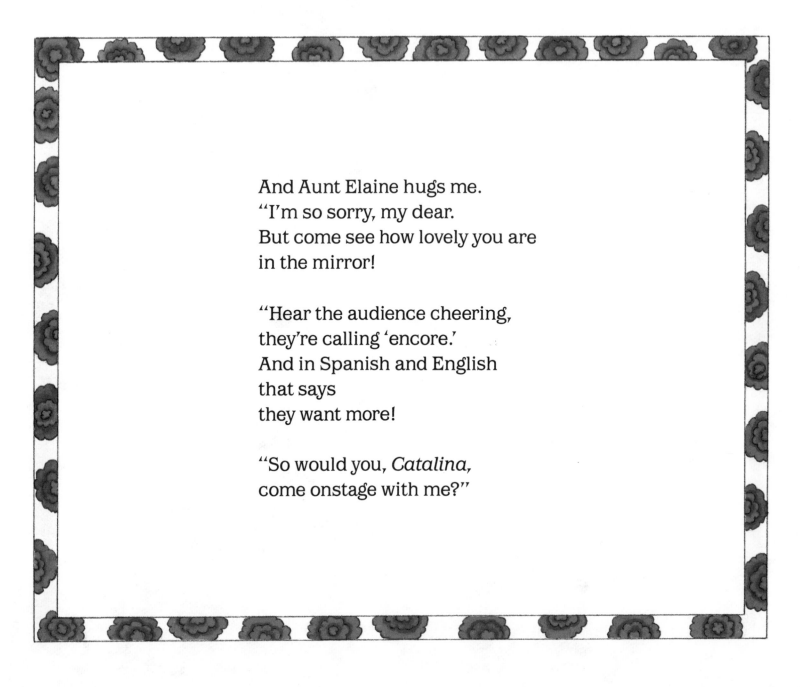

And Aunt Elaine hugs me.
"I'm so sorry, my dear.
But come see how lovely you are
in the mirror!

"Hear the audience cheering,
they're calling 'encore.'
And in Spanish and English
that says
they want more!

"So would you, *Catalina,*
come onstage with me?"

LEAH KOMAIKO is the author of several popular books for children, including *Annie Bananie* and *I Like the Music. Aunt Elaine Does the Dance from Spain* is her first book for Doubleday. Although Leah Komaiko does not really have an aunt Elaine, she does have a sister who is a famous Spanish dancer and choreographer.

PETRA MATHERS is the author and illustrator of *Maria Theresa, Theodor and Mr. Balbini,* and *Sophie and Lou,* none of whom know how to do the dance from Spain. She intends to be a glamorous grandmother when the time comes.

The illustrations were prepared on 300 lb. Arches cold-press watercolor paper using watercolors and pencil.

The book is set in 15 pt. ITG Barcelona, a new typeface designed by Ed Benguiat. Typography by Lynn Braswell.